Jingle Bells

To my father, Samuel Kovalski

First U.S. edition

First published in Canada by Kids Can Press

Originally published in 1859 as "Jingle Bells or the One Horse Open Sleigh, Song and Chorus," by J. Pierpont.

ISBN 0-316-50258-8

Library of Congress Catalog Card Number 88—45474

Joy Street Books are published by
Little, Brown and Company (Inc.)

10 9 8 7 6 5 4 3 2 1

Printed and bound by Everbest Printing Co. Ltd., Hong Kong

Maryann Kovalski

Jingle Bells

Joy Street Books
Little, Brown and Company
Boston   Toronto

Jenny and Joanna woke up early. It was a very special morning. Grandma was taking them on a trip! They were going to stay in a big hotel, just the three of them.

When Grandma arrived, they all piled into a taxi and sped off to the airport.

Jenny and Joanna had never been on an airplane before.
"I want to see everything," said Jenny. "Can we meet the pilot?"

"Yes, yes," said Grandma, "but first, here comes breakfast."

It was almost dark by the time they got off the plane and arrived at the hotel, but they weren't tired at all.

"Oh, look, Grandma," said Joanna, "there's a horse and carriage. Can we go for a ride?"

"Please, Grandma," said Jenny.

"Okay," laughed Grandma, "but we'll have to bundle up."

They chose the biggest and shiniest carriage of them all.

"Evening, ladies," the driver said, tipping his hat. "Ready for a spin through the park?"

Off they went! It was quiet in the park, and the tinkling of the little bells on the horse's harness filled the air.

"Let's sing!" Grandma said.

Refrain

Jin - gle bells, jin - gle bells, jin - gle all the way!

Joanna, Jenny and Grandma sang at the top of their lungs. The driver sang loudest of all.

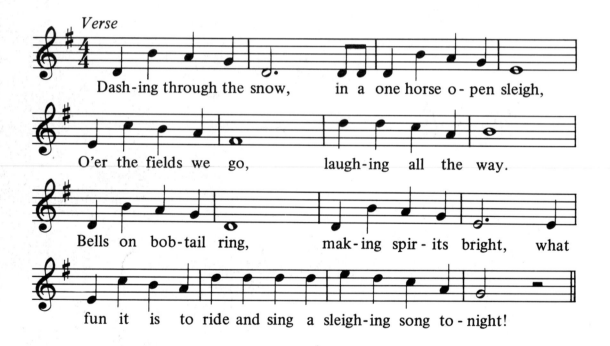

Verse

Dash-ing through the snow, in a one horse o-pen sleigh,

O'er the fields we go, laugh-ing all the way.

Bells on bob-tail ring, mak-ing spir-its bright, what

fun it is to ride and sing a sleigh-ing song to-night!

Ohhhhhhhhhhhhhhhhhhhhhhh . . .

Suddenly, the driver was gone!

"Oh, no!" they screamed.

With no one driving, the horse took off at full speed.
Just as the carriage was about to topple, Grandma
lunged into the driver's seat and grabbed the reins.

"Whoa!" she cried.

The horse slowed to a trot.

"Don't worry," she said, "everything is under control."

"Then let's keep going, Grandma!" Jenny and Joanna
shouted.

They headed out of the park onto the street,
waving at everyone they saw.

Refrain

Jin - gle bells,   jin - gle bells,   jin - gle all   the way!

Oh what fun   it is   to ride in a one horse o - pen   sleigh!___

Jin - gle bells,   jin - gle bells,   jin - gle all   the way!

Oh what fun   it   is   to ride in a one horse o - pen sleigh!

Suddenly, the traffic was going in the wrong direction. "Grandma, where are we going?" Joanna asked.

There was shouting and honking and
confusion all around.

"Oh dear," said Grandma.

"Now what will we do?" asked Jenny.

Grandma climbed out of the carriage.
"Don't worry!" she said, spying a bright red truck in front of them. "I know just what to do."

And she did.

"All aboard, ladies!" the truck driver said.

Before they knew it, they were in the bright red
truck and on their way back to their hotel. And
if you listened very carefully you could hear
three tired but happy voices singing . . .

Jin-gle b

The End